Make a Masterpiece

Pen and Ink

by Alix Wood

Gareth Stevens PUBLISHING

Please visit our website, www.garethstevens.com. For a free color catalog of all our high-quality books, call toll free 1-800-542-2595 or fax 1-877-542-2596

Cataloging-in-Publication Data

Names: Wood, Alix.
Title: Pen and ink / Alix Wood.
Description: New York : Gareth Stevens Publishing, 2019. | Series: Make a masterpiece | Includes glossary and index.
Identifiers: ISBN 9781538235805 (pbk.) | ISBN 9781538235928 (library bound) | ISBN 9781538235843 (6pack)
Subjects: LCSH: Pen drawing--Technique--Juvenile literature.
Classification: LCC NC905.W66 2019 | DDC 741.2'6--dc23

First Edition

Published in 2019 by
Gareth Stevens Publishing
111 East 14th Street, Suite 349
New York, NY 10003

Produced for Gareth Stevens by Alix Wood Books
Designed by Alix Wood
Editor: Eloise Macgregor
Consultant: Richard Mabey, ink and watercolor artist

Photo credits:
Cover and title page background, 5 top © Adobe Stock Images;
4 © public domain; all other images © Alix Wood

Printed in the United States of America

CPSIA compliance information: Batch #CW19GS For further information contact Gareth Stevens, New York, New York at 1-800-542-2595.

Contents

Making Art with Pen and Ink 4
Ways of Using Ink 6
Shading with Texture 8
Creating Fur Texture 10
Project Page: Crazy Hand 12
Comic Illustrations 14
Project Page: Make a Cartoon Card 16
Fun with Type 18
Project Page: Graffiti Letters 20
Design with Doodles 22
Project Page: Draw a Zentangle® 24
Painting with Ink 26
Project Page: Ink Wash Chickens 28
Glossary 30
Further Information 31
Index 32

Making Art with Pen and Ink

The great thing about pen and ink is that all you need is a pen (or even a stick) and a piece of paper, and you're ready to make some great art! The strong line that ink makes can create some amazing pictures. You can paint using ink, too. If you add water to black ink, you can create different **tints** and **shades** of gray. And ink isn't just black. You can get ink in every color of the rainbow!

Pen and ink is often used for book illustrations, as it is cheaper to print using just black ink. This pen and ink illustration is from *The Story of King Arthur and His Knights* by the artist Howard Pyle.

What Will You Need?

Ink described as "permanent" means it won't fade. It does not mean it is waterproof.

Types of Ink

It is best to have two different types of black ink, one that is waterproof, and one that isn't. Waterproof ink won't smudge when you paint over it. Non-waterproof ink is great for blending hard edges and using with a brush.

Different Pens

Markers are good for bold outlines and covering areas quickly. A blue ballpoint pen is great for **doodling**, or drawing clouds, the sea, or anything blue. A technical drawing pen draws neat outlines, and most contain waterproof ink. Sticks and nib pens can create both thick and thin lines by using different angles or pressure.

Paper

Smooth paper works best with pen and ink. Most standard sketch pads will work well.

Adding Color

In this book, we use watercolor pencils to add color to many of the projects. They are easy to use and are great for drawing detail. You could also use colored inks if you have them.

Brushes

A large and a small watercolor brush will be useful for applying ink or adding color.

You will also need paper towels, a pencil, an eraser, and old clothes. Remember, ink will stain, so be careful!

Ways of Using Ink

You can draw, print, and paint using ink. Using black ink on its own creates a strong image. Ink is great for drawing an outline to color in. It is also perfect for adding detail at the final stage of your art.

Ink stains! Wear old clothes and protect your work area.

Making Different Marks

TIP Try moving your pen or stick in different directions to create different marks. Press lightly, and then press harder and watch how the marks change. If you have colored inks, try drawing with them using a stick.

Master Class

Make Your Own Brush

You can easily make your own ink brushes. Collect objects that you think might make interesting marks. Remember that the ink will stain, so don't use anything valuable! Taping your objects onto a stick may make them easier to use.

Shading with Texture

If your ink is black and your paper is white, how can you draw grays using pen and ink? It's easy! You create the **illusion** of light and dark by using **shading** and **texture**. There are several different ways to shade your drawing using an ink pen. Try the exercises on these pages, and learn some cool pen-and-ink tricks.

Draw five simple balls on some paper. Decide where your light is coming from. The other side will be in shadow. Shade each ball in a different way.

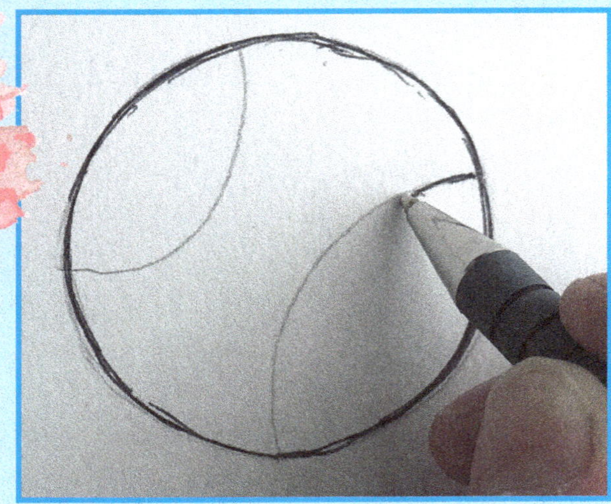

Hatching

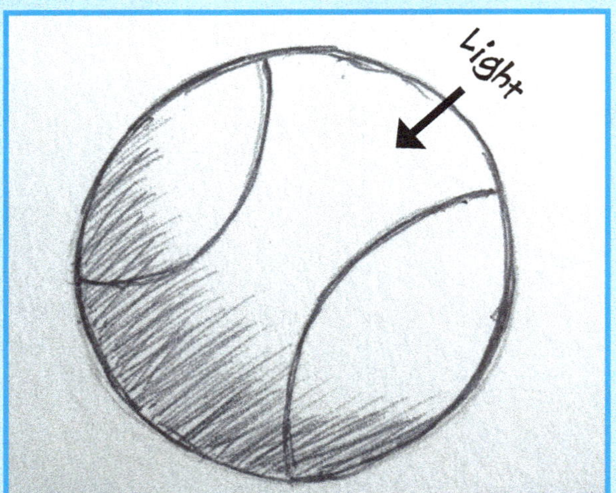

Our light is coming from the top right-hand corner. Start drawing some lines to shade the opposite side of your ball.

Add some shorter lines around the edge of the shaded side of the ball, to make that area look even darker.

Crosshatching

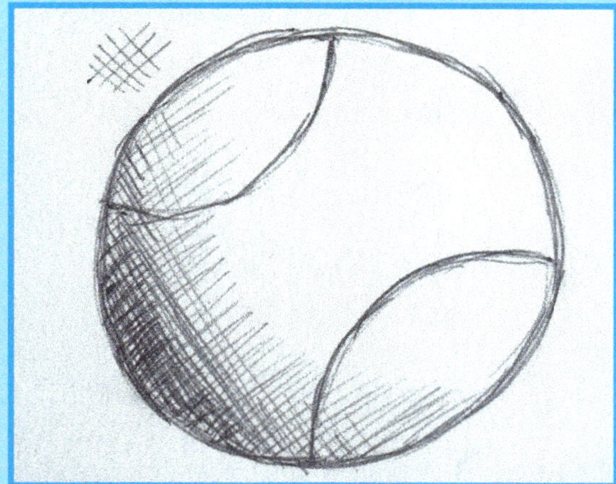

Draw hatching lines. Then add lines going across for the darker shading areas.

Directional Lines

Draw lines that follow the shape of the object that you are shading.

Scribbling

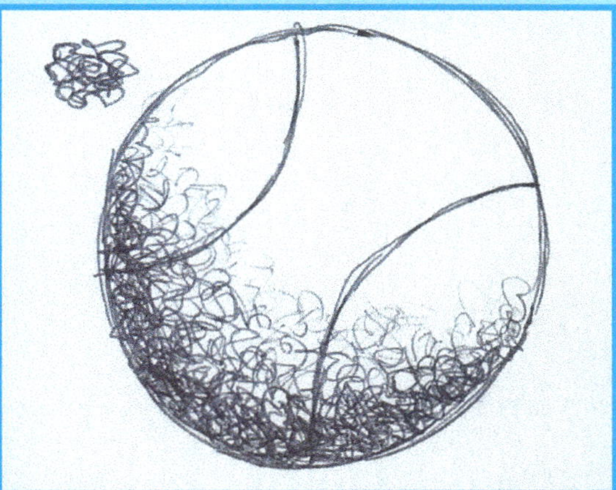

Draw **random** squiggles to shade your ball.

Stippling

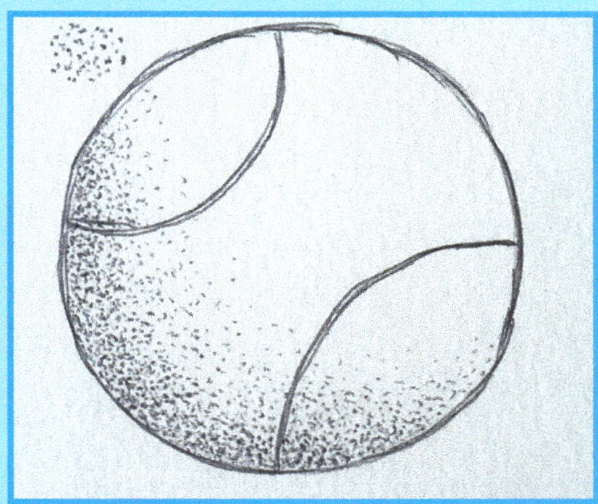

Shade using dots.

Creating Fur Texture

Try this project using your new shading techniques. Use directional lines to draw fur on this pony. Then use dots to shade the pony's skin around its **muzzle**.

1

Using pencil, draw a large and small circle, and join them together as shown. Add ears and a neck to complete your pony's head.

2

Add the pony's mane, eye, nostrils, mouth, and **bridle** as shown.

3

Go over your pencil lines using an ink pen. Then erase your pencil. Don't use ballpoint as the eraser will smudge the lines.

TIP

It is a good idea to wash your hands before using pen and ink. Oil on your hands and fingers can transfer to the paper and cause the ink to blur or look blotchy.

4

Start to shade your pony using directional lines. Look at photographs of ponies to see the direction their fur grows. Draw your ink lines in the correct direction to get realistic-looking fur.

5

Make the inside of the ears nice and dark, as they would be in shadow. Leave some areas free of lines. These highlights show where the light is hitting the pony.

Ink in the eyes and nostril. Add some stippled dots to the pony's muzzle to complete your picture.

Project Page:

Crazy Hand

Have fun exploring different textures to create this amazing, crazy-looking hand. It's easy to do and is great practice for your ink techniques. You can use any kind of pen for this project. We used an ordinary blue ballpoint.

1

Draw around your hand using a ballpoint.

2

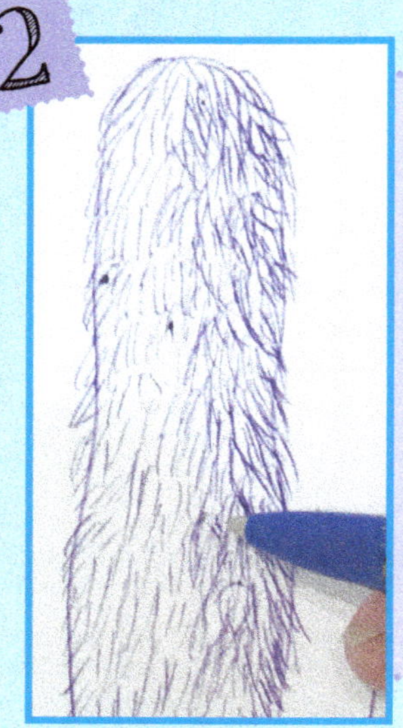

Choose a finger for your furry texture. Draw short lines in the direction you want the fur to grow. Imagine the light is coming from the left, so make the right side darker by adding more lines.

3

Draw sausages all down another finger. Shade the bottom of each sausage using curving lines. Make the right side darker.

4

Start at the bottom of another finger and draw overlapping pine-cone shapes. Shade the bottom of each shape.

5

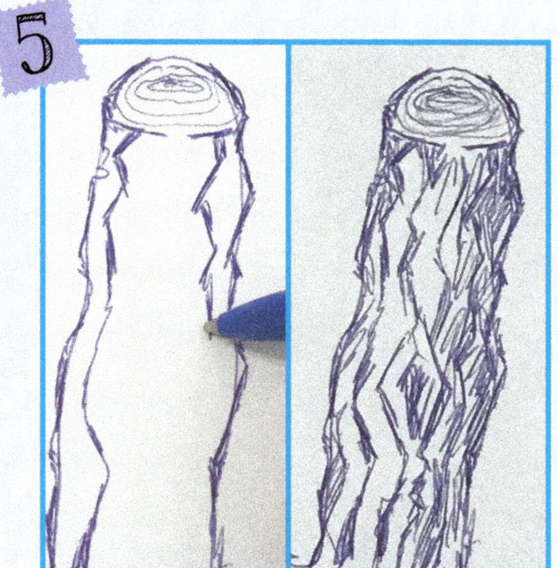

On your fourth finger, draw a few circles at the top to look like chopped wood. Then create your bark by drawing dark, jagged lines. Make the right side darker.

6

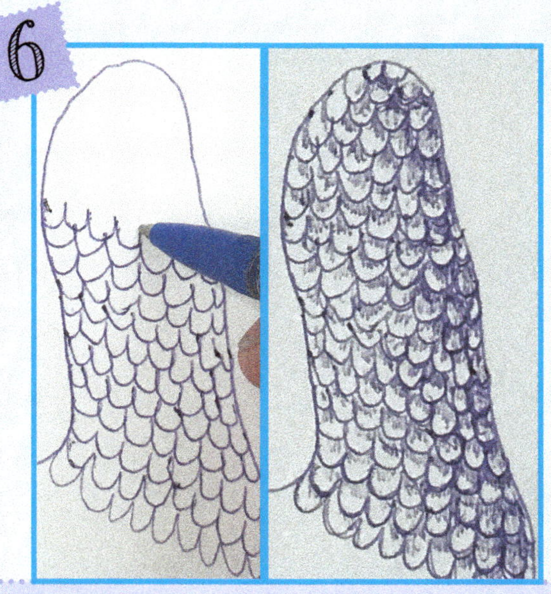

To create your scaly thumb, start at the bottom and draw a row of "U" shapes. Then draw more rows to fill your thumb. Shade the top of each scale, getting darker on the right side.

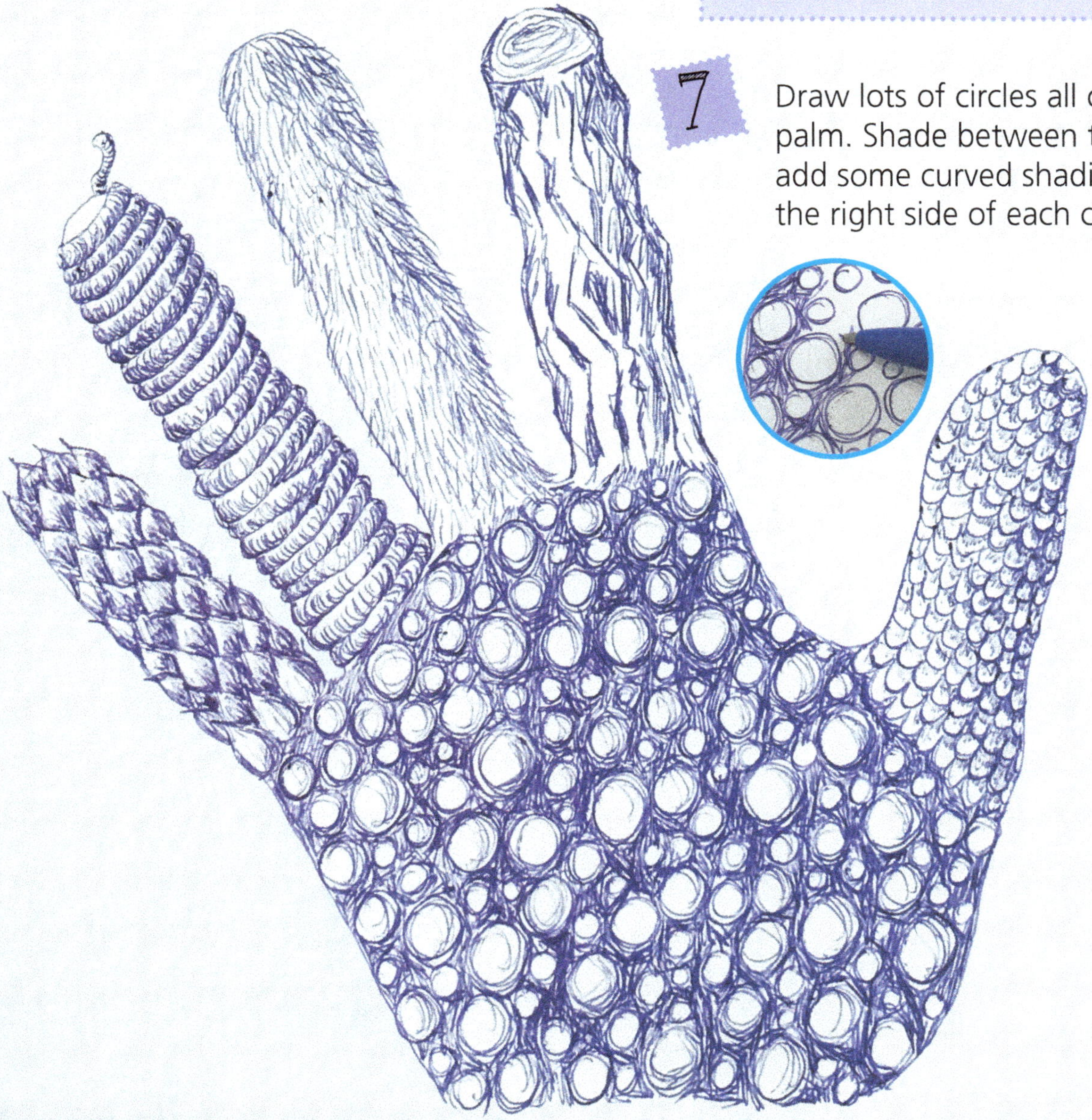

7

Draw lots of circles all over your palm. Shade between them and add some curved shading on the right side of each circle.

Comic Illustrations

Pen and ink is perfect for creating cartoons and comic books. You can create many different animals from a basic egg shape. Try it yourself. We used a black marker to create these cartoons.

How to Draw a Simple Cartoon Cat

1

Draw a simple egg shape.

2

Add some pointy ears, two eyes, and a small nose and mouth.

3

Then add some whiskers, four legs, and a tail.

Try Some More Animals...

Using the same basic egg shape, you can create a hamster...

... or a dog,

... or a penguin.

TIP

When drawing an egg shape, it can be hard to get the sides to look the same. Your drawing hand covers the line you are trying to match. Try turning the paper upside down when you draw the awkward side.

Master Class

Changing Expressions

With just a few simple changes to the eyes, you can make your egg character have all kinds of different expressions.

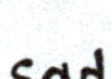

sad

tired

happy

angry

Try adding drooping ears, whiskers, and arms to make your character look really sad, or really tired.

Make your angry hamster shake his fists and stamp his foot!

Dancing feet and waving wings will make your penguin look happy.

PROJECT PAGE:

Make a Cartoon Card

Use your new comic characters from page 14 to make a cartoon card. You'll need a rectangle of thin card or good watercolor paper, a marker, and some paint or colored pencils to color your card in with.

1

Fold your paper in half to make a card. Lightly sketch a banner, and three overlapping egg shapes on the front of your card. Draw a cake halfway down the front egg.

2

Add details to the eggs to turn them into your cartoon characters from pages 14 and 15. Add some candles to the cake.

3

When you are happy with your design, go over your pencil lines using a marker. Then erase your pencil lines.

4

On the inside of your card, draw another character enjoying a slice of cake. Color in your character. We used some watercolor pencils.

5

Color in the front of your card.

Write your chosen celebration onto the banner, and your card is ready to go.

Fun with Type

In the **Middle Ages**, before the **printing press** was invented, books were handwritten works of art. The first letter of a page was often decorated using colorful inks or even very thin pieces of real gold and silver. Try designing your own decorated letter.

1

Using pencil, draw a letter with a frame around it. Go over the lines in ink, and then erase the pencil.

Ballpoint pen may smudge when you erase your pencil. Just leave the pencil and color over it later.

2

Add some simple pencil designs to the frame and the background.

3

Once you are happy with your design, go over your pencil using ink and then erase the pencil.

Now you can color in your decorated letter. We used some watercolor pencils for ours.

If you used watercolor pencils, you can turn the pencil marks into paint using a damp brush.

Wash your brush after each color you paint, otherwise the colors will mix and look muddy. Here's our finished letter.

TIP

If the ink you used wasn't waterproof, use colored pencils instead of watercolor pencils, or skip step 5 and don't use any water with them. Otherwise, your ink will smudge and ruin your picture.

Project Page:

Graffiti Letters

Draw **three-dimensional** letters and your favorite possession inside a colored outline to create a cool design of your own name.

How to Draw a 3-D Letter

First draw an outline of your letter. Graffiti letters are usually chunky, like this letter M above.

Now make it look like a solid 3-D shape. Draw short angled lines from any right hand corners of your letter shape.

Join your corner lines together. You may need to add other straight lines in some places, see arrow.

1

Create your name in 3-D letters. Outline your name. Add a favorite object, and then put another outline around your whole design.

2

You could add a cool brick design behind your graffiti.

3

Go over your pencil lines using waterproof ink. We used a technical drawing pen.

4

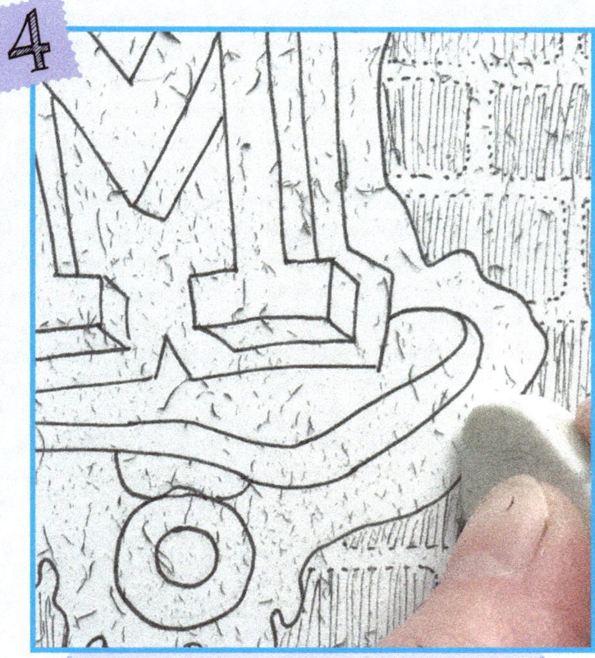

Use hatching to shade your bricks. Then erase your pencil lines.

We used watercolor pencils to color our graffiti design. Remember to wash your brush between colors and paint from light to dark to keep the light colors looking clean and bright.

Design with Doodles

Do you doodle? Doodles are those little pictures or patterns you draw when you are bored or thinking about something else. You can make some great designs and fun pieces of art using simple ballpoint doodles. Try drawing zigzags, spirals, stars, heart shapes, and circles. Add some wavy lines, dotted lines, dashes, and swirls!

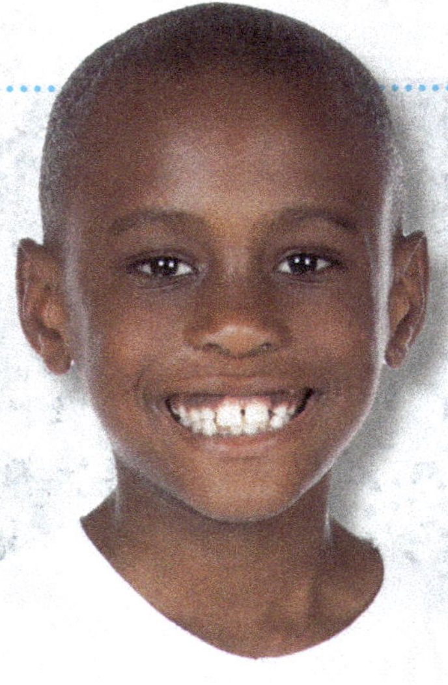

TIP

If you have some fabric pens, you could design your own doodle T-shirt. Fabric pens are specially designed not to run or smudge when clothes are washed. Ordinary ballpoint will not wash very well, and might stain other clothes in the wash, too. Practice your design on a piece of paper before you draw it onto your T-shirt.

Master Class

Doodle Picture

Make some doodle art. You will need some paper and a few different-colored ballpoint pens or thin markers.

Draw a shape or a word in the center of your paper. Fill it and surround it with all your fun doodles.

PROJECT PAGE:

Draw a Zentangle®

Try this fun scribble doodle project. It is very relaxing! These type of drawings are known as Zentangles®. Zen is a type of **meditation**, where people focus their minds on an activity to help them feel calm and think clearly. The "tangle" is the random line you make to start your drawing. Your tangled line should look as if you have dropped a length of string on the floor. Try making a Zentangle® and see if it relaxes you.

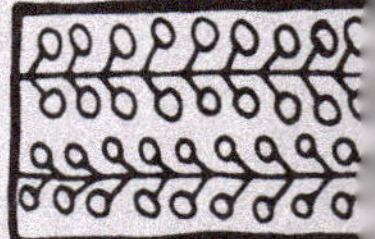
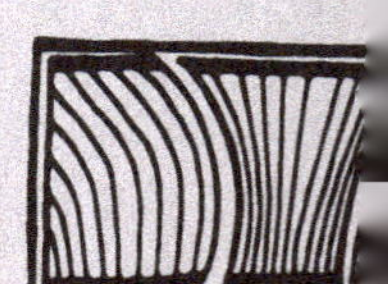
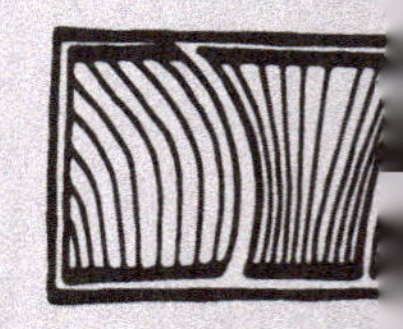

1

Draw a curving, overlapping line all over your paper. You want to create shapes you can fill in with doodles.

2

Start to fill each section of your scribble drawing. Use some of the doodles you practiced on pages 22 and 23.

TIP

To get some inspiration, have a look at some coloring books and Zentangle® books. See what shapes and patterns other people have used to fill their spaces. You can make your own Zentangle® library of little squares to refer to.

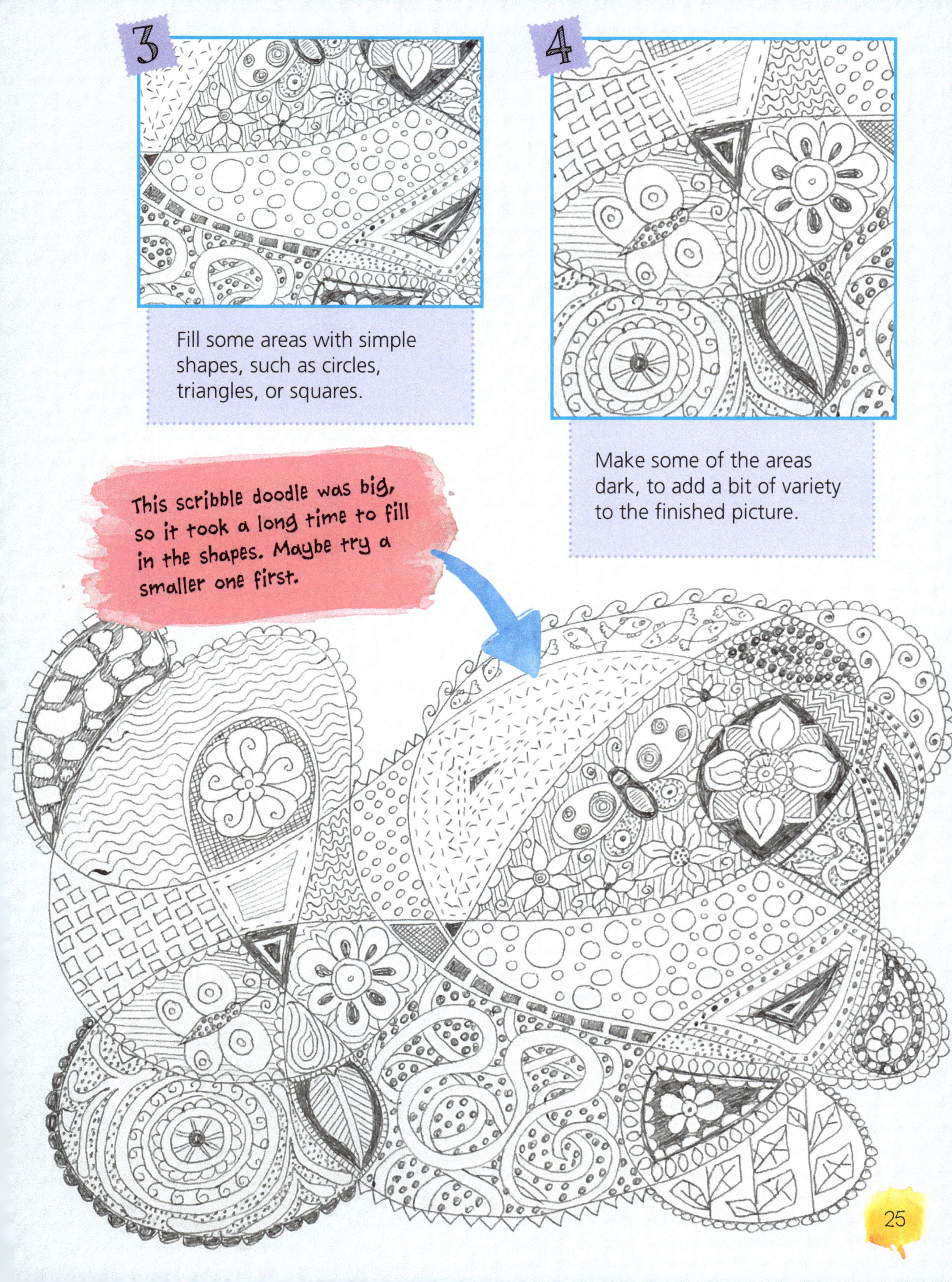

Fill some areas with simple shapes, such as circles, triangles, or squares.

Make some of the areas dark, to add a bit of variety to the finished picture.

Painting with Ink

You can use ink to paint with, just as you would with watercolor paint. You can use it straight out of the bottle, and you can add water to it. Practice the skills on this page and learn how to add ink shading to your ink line pictures. You will need ink, water, a mixing **palette** and paintbrush, and a sheet of watercolor paper.

Bleeds

Wet your paper and dab some ink on using a paintbrush. You can get some great effects.

Making Different Tints of Ink

Using a brush, transfer some ink into one compartment of a mixing palette. Then quickly dip your brush in and out of some water.

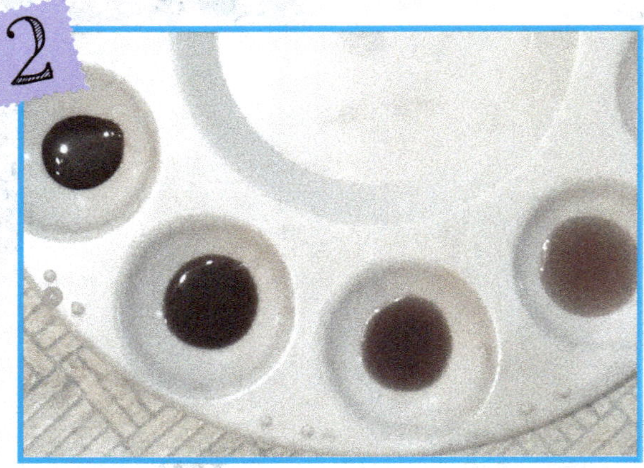

Transfer your brush full of watery ink into the next compartment. Repeat until you have around six different tints of ink from very dark to very light. Paint a square in each tint to see how they look.

Master Class

Paint a Graded Ink Wash

To paint a background of gradually fading gray, try adding water to your ink as you paint, to gradually lighten the color.

1

This **graded wash** goes from dark to light. Prop your paper at a slight slope, so the ink will slowly run down the paper. Start with a dark tint. Paint a couple of broad stripes across the top of your paper.

2

Lightly dip your inky brush in water, and then paint a couple more stripes under the dark one.

3

Continue down the paper, adding water until the tint is very light. Try adding some trees using one of your homemade brushes and a dark tint of ink. Use the stick end to draw the tree trunks.

PROJECT PAGE:

Ink Wash Chickens

Traditional Japanese artists used ink outlines and shading with dashes of color to create their art. Try this Japanese-inspired painting. You will need to use waterproof ink for your outlines, so the ink doesn't run when you add your shading.

1

Draw a rooster and hen lightly using pencil. Draw egg shapes for their bodies, then add the heads, tails, and legs. Add a couple of little egg-shaped chicks, too.

2

Once you are happy with your drawing, go over the outline of your chickens in waterproof ink. We used a hen's feather to draw our outlines!

3

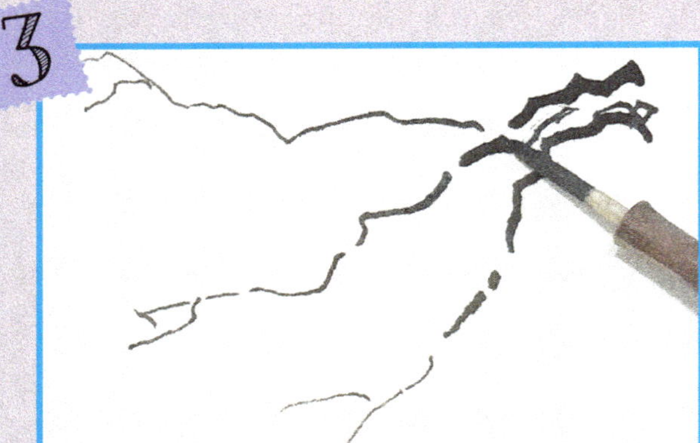

We used a stick to draw our branch. Twist and turn the stick as you make your marks. This creates interesting angles and breaks in your line.

4

Take a small paintbrush and add the red details to the tree blossom and the chickens' heads. You can use red ink or paint.

5

Using a clean, small paintbrush, add areas of gray ink wash to the shadowy areas of your picture. Add some detail to the rooster's tail, and some rough grass.

Glossary

bridle A device for controlling a horse made up of a set of straps enclosing the head, a bit, and a pair of reins.

buckle To develop kinks and bend out of shape.

doodling Scribbling a sketch or design while thinking of something else.

graded wash A thin layer of paint where the color goes from pale to dark or dark to pale.

illusion A misleading image.

meditation The act of spending time quietly thinking.

Middle Ages The period of European history from about AD 500 to about 1500.

muzzle The nose and jaws of an animal.

palette A board or dish used by a painter to lay and mix paint colors on.

printing press A machine that produces printed copies.

random Without definite aim, direction, rule, or method.

shades The darkness or lightness of a color.

shading The darkening of some objects in a painting or drawing to suggest that they are in shade.

texture The structure, feel, and appearance of something.

three-dimensional Giving the appearance of depth.

tints Shades or varieties of a color.

Further Information

Books

Davis, Rich. *The 1-Minute Artist: Learn to Draw Almost Anything in Six Easy Steps.* New York, NY: Race Point Publishing, 2016.

Johnson, Clare. *How to Draw.* New York, NY: DK Children, 2017.

Websites

Art is Fun website with information about pen and ink drawing:
www.art-is-fun.com/pen-and-ink-drawings/

This website shows you how to make a quill pen using a straw:
www.pinkstripeysocks.com/2013/06/make-quill-pens-out-of-straws-and-dye.html

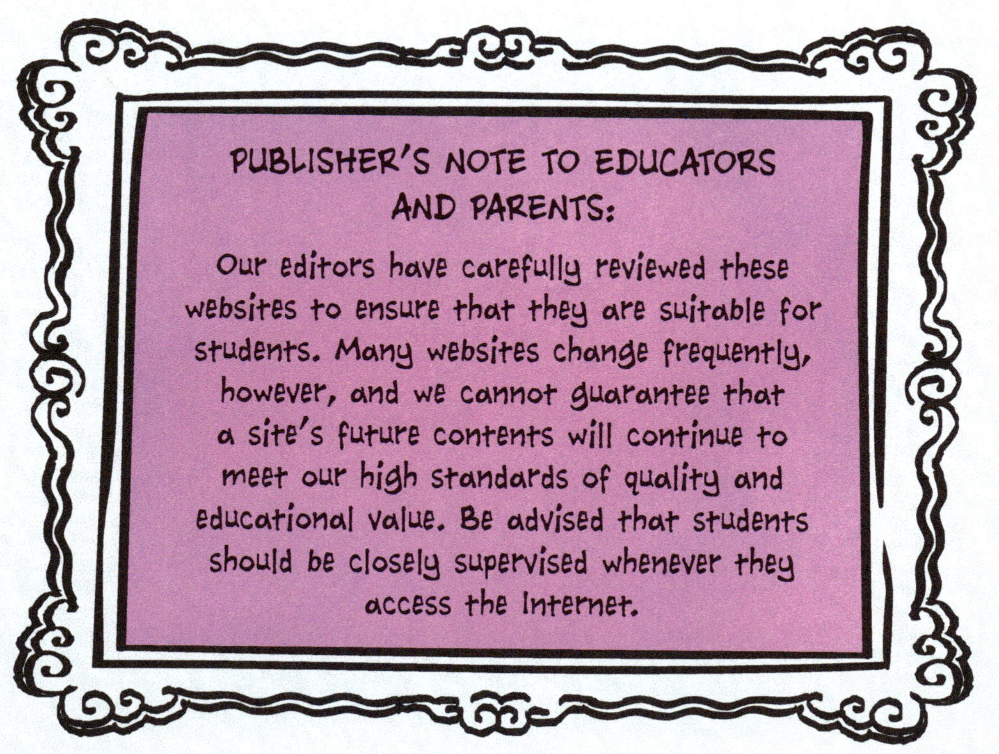

Index

B
ballpoint pens 5, 7, 12, 22, 23
brushes 5, 6, 7, 26, 27, 29

C
cartoons 14, 15, 16, 17
colored ink 4
crosshatching 9

D
decorated letters 18, 19
directional lines 9, 13
doodles 5, 22, 23

F
fabric pens 22
fur 10, 11

G
graffiti letters 20, 21

H
hatching 8, 9

I
illustrations 4

M
markers 5, 6, 14

N
nib pens 6

P
paper 5, 26
Pyle, Howard 4

S
scribbling 9
shading 8, 9, 10, 11, 12, 13, 29
smudging 5, 10, 18, 19, 28
staining 7, 22, 28
sticks 6, 28
stippling 9, 11

T
technical pens 5, 6, 21
textures 10, 11, 12, 13
tints 26, 27

W
washes 27
watercolor pencils 5, 17, 19, 21

Z
Zentangles® 24, 25